The Little Red Hen

Story by Nikki Gamble
Illustrated by Scott Nash

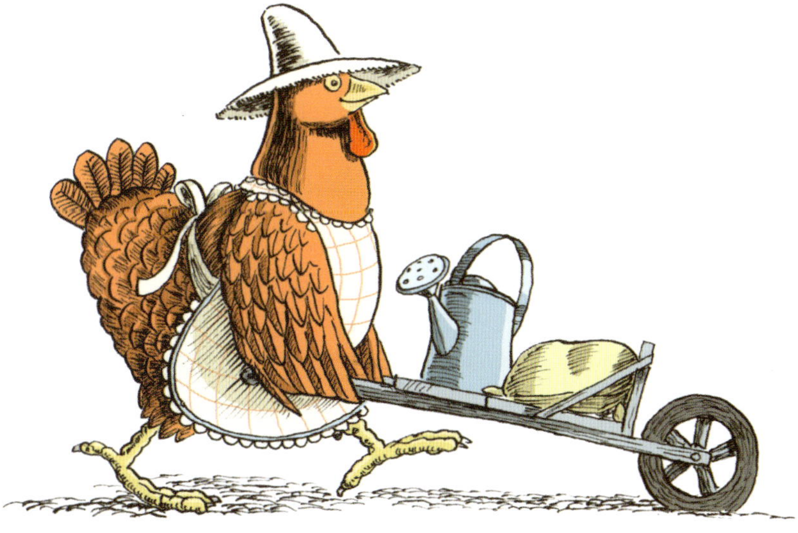

OXFORD
UNIVERSITY PRESS

W0051217

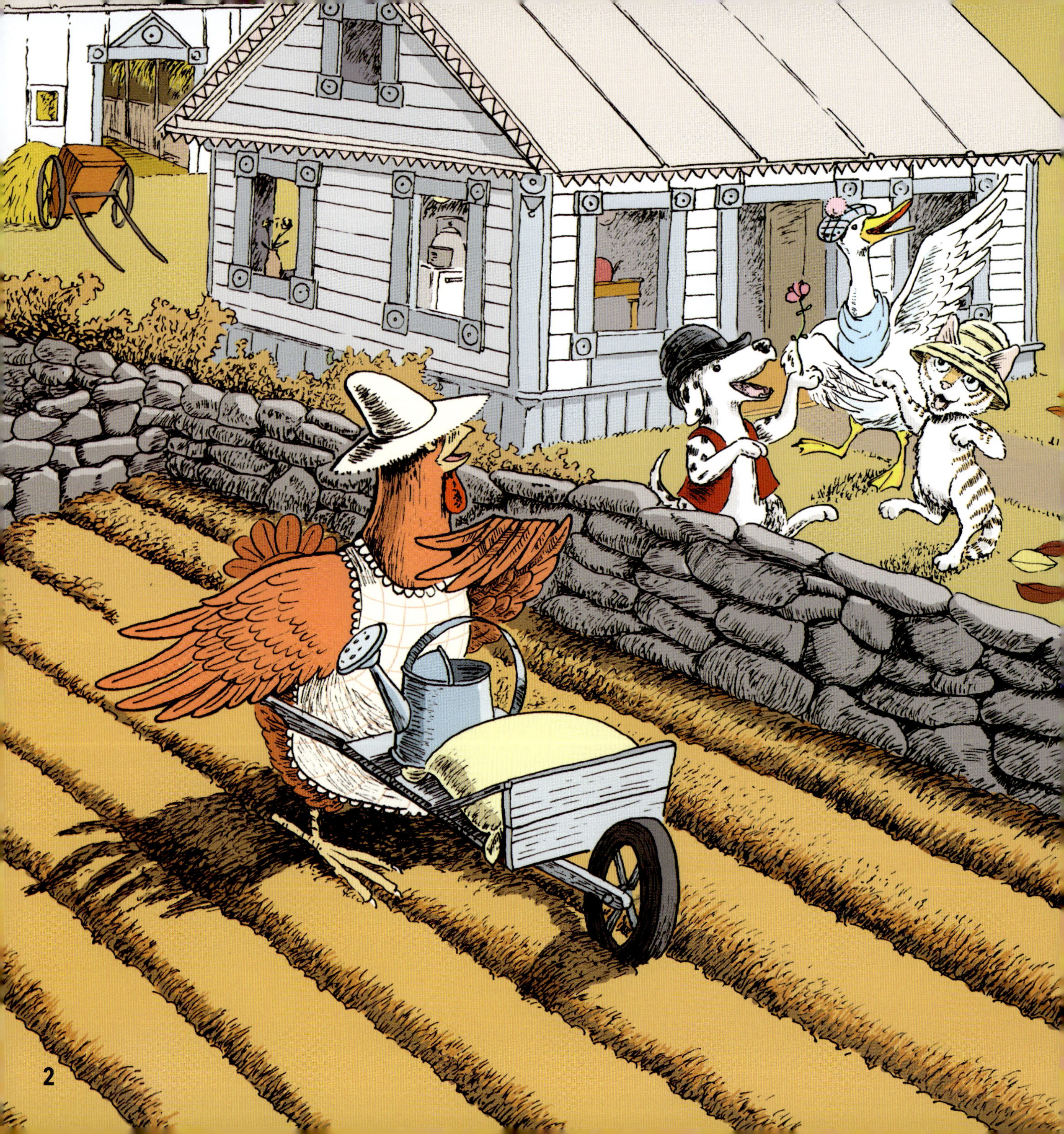

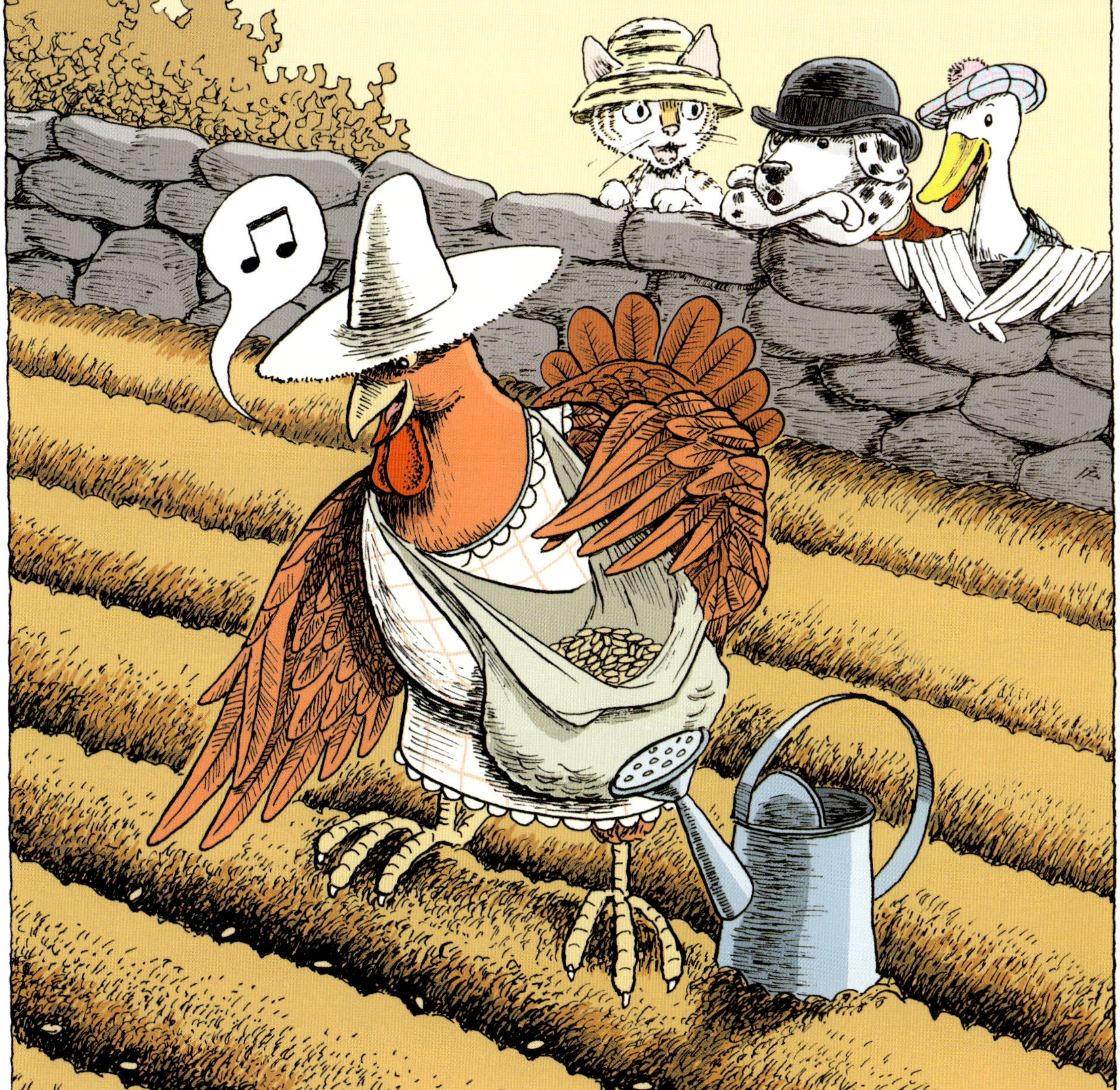

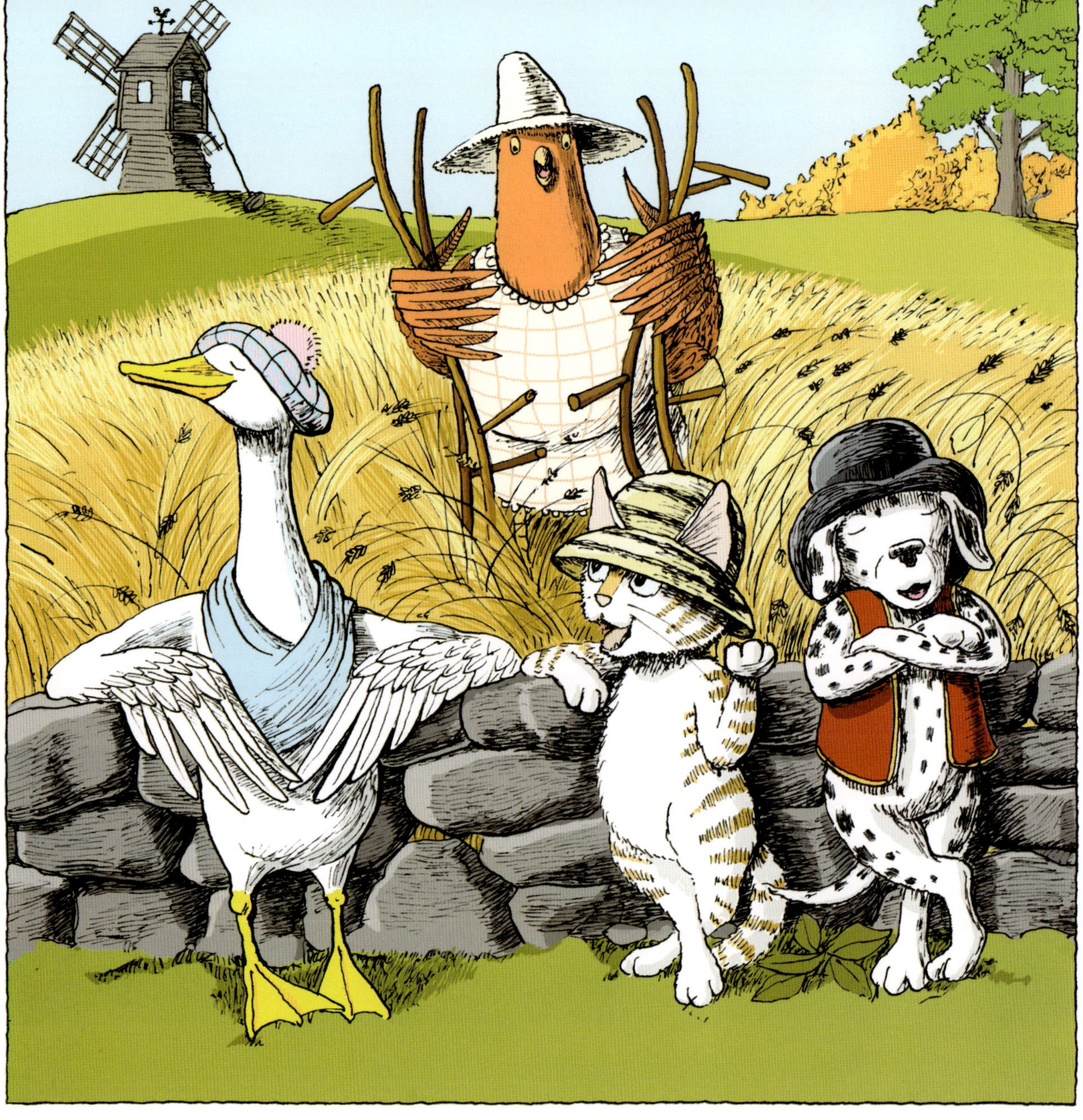

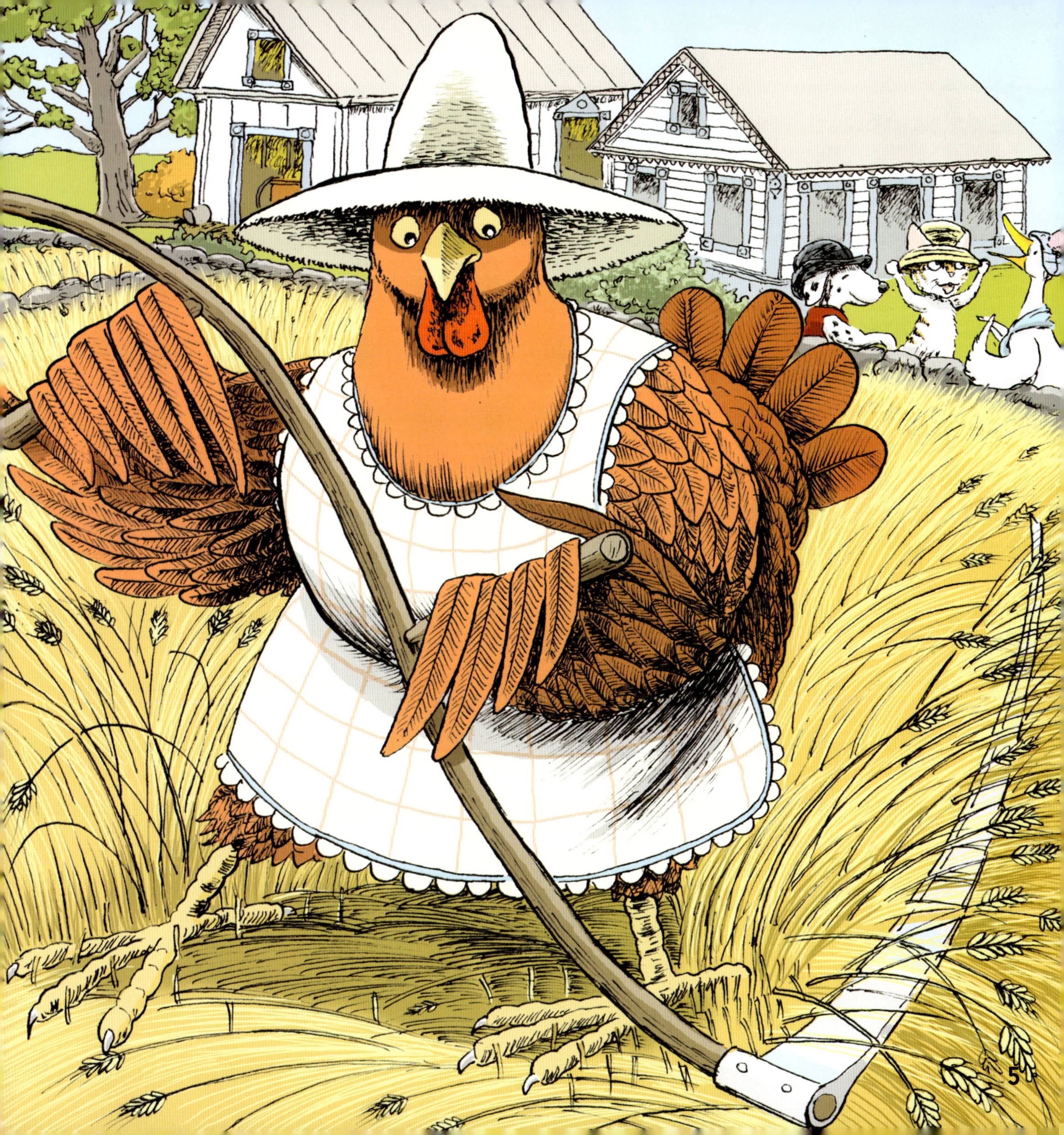

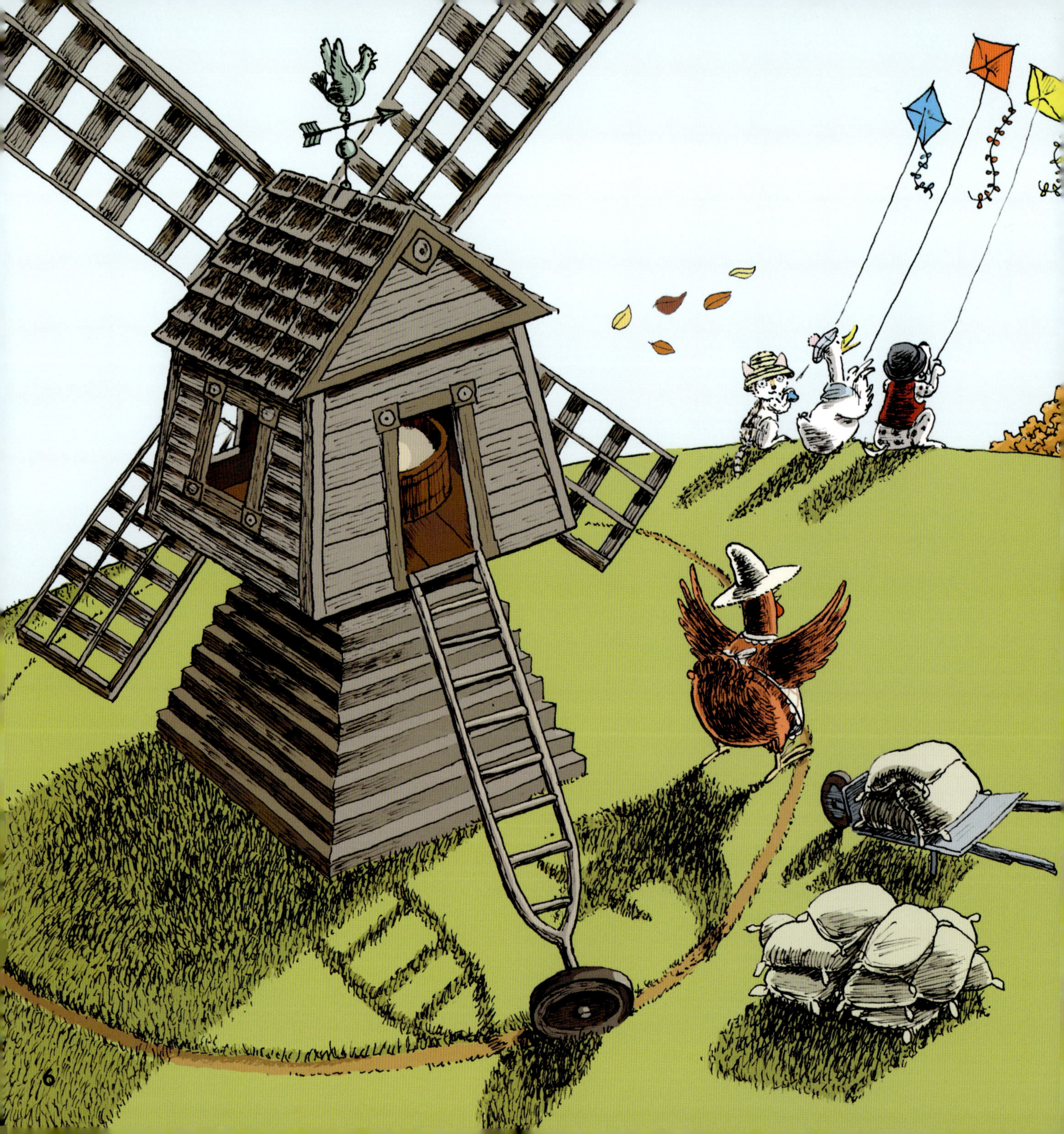

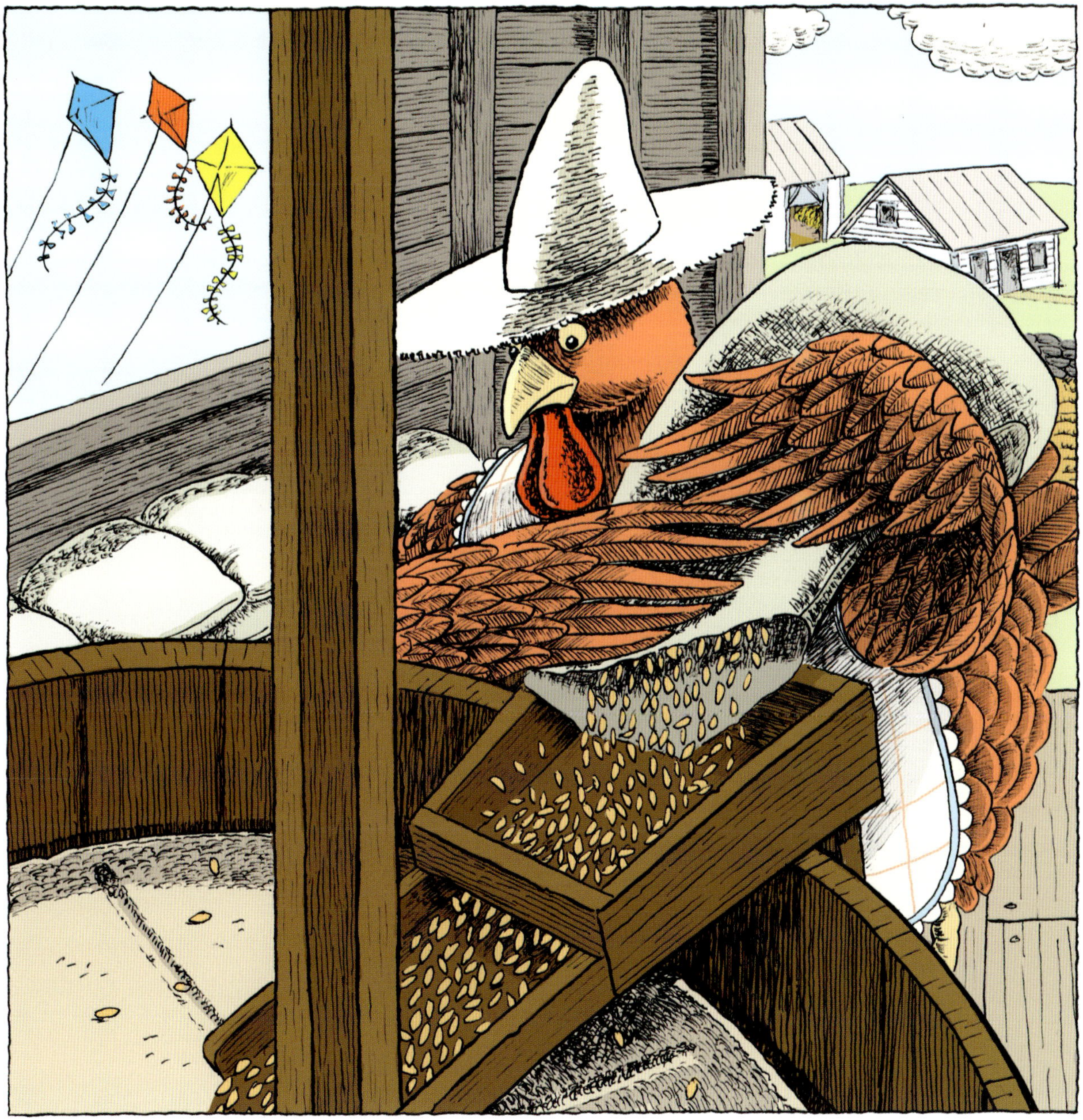

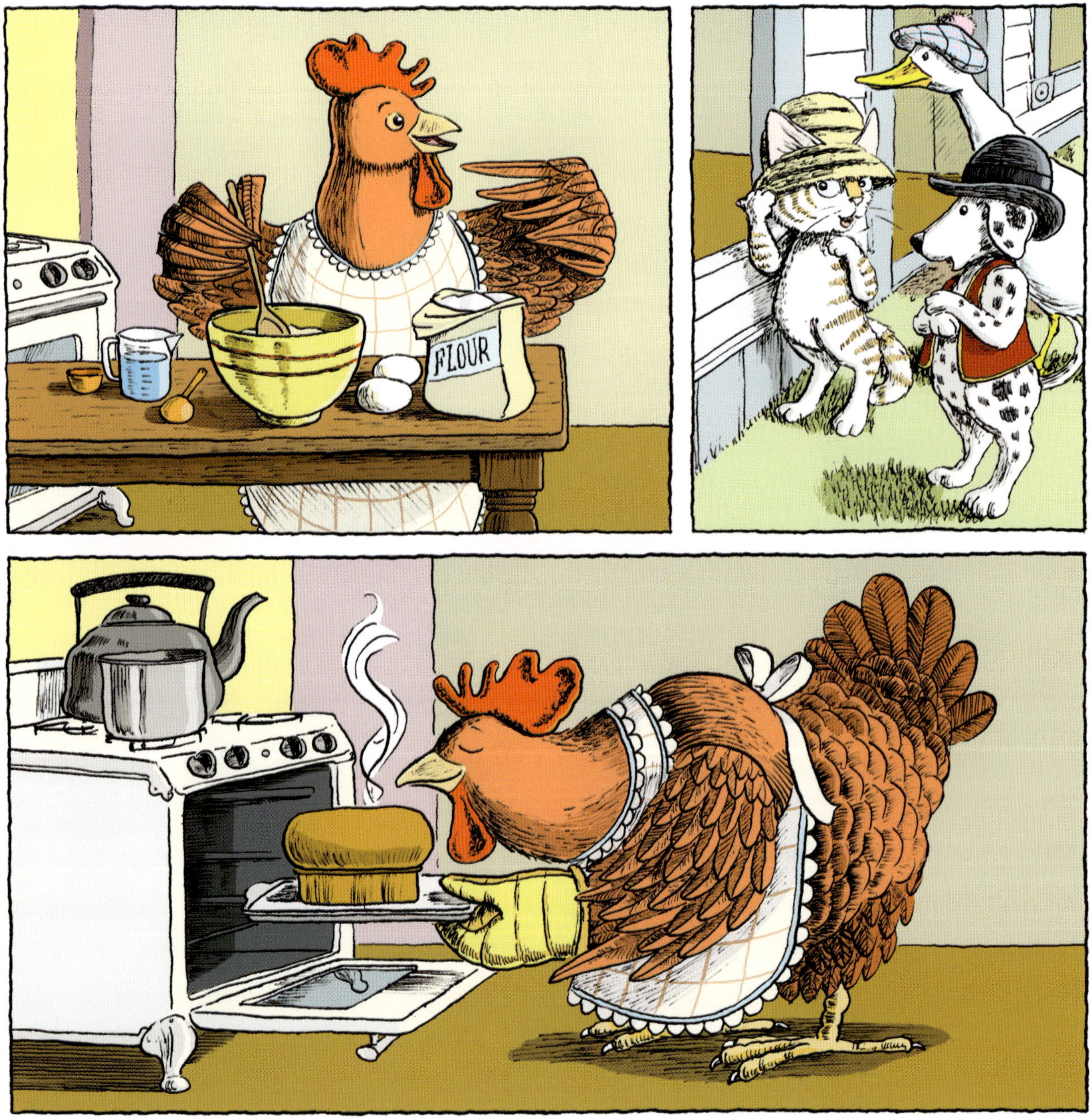
FLOUR

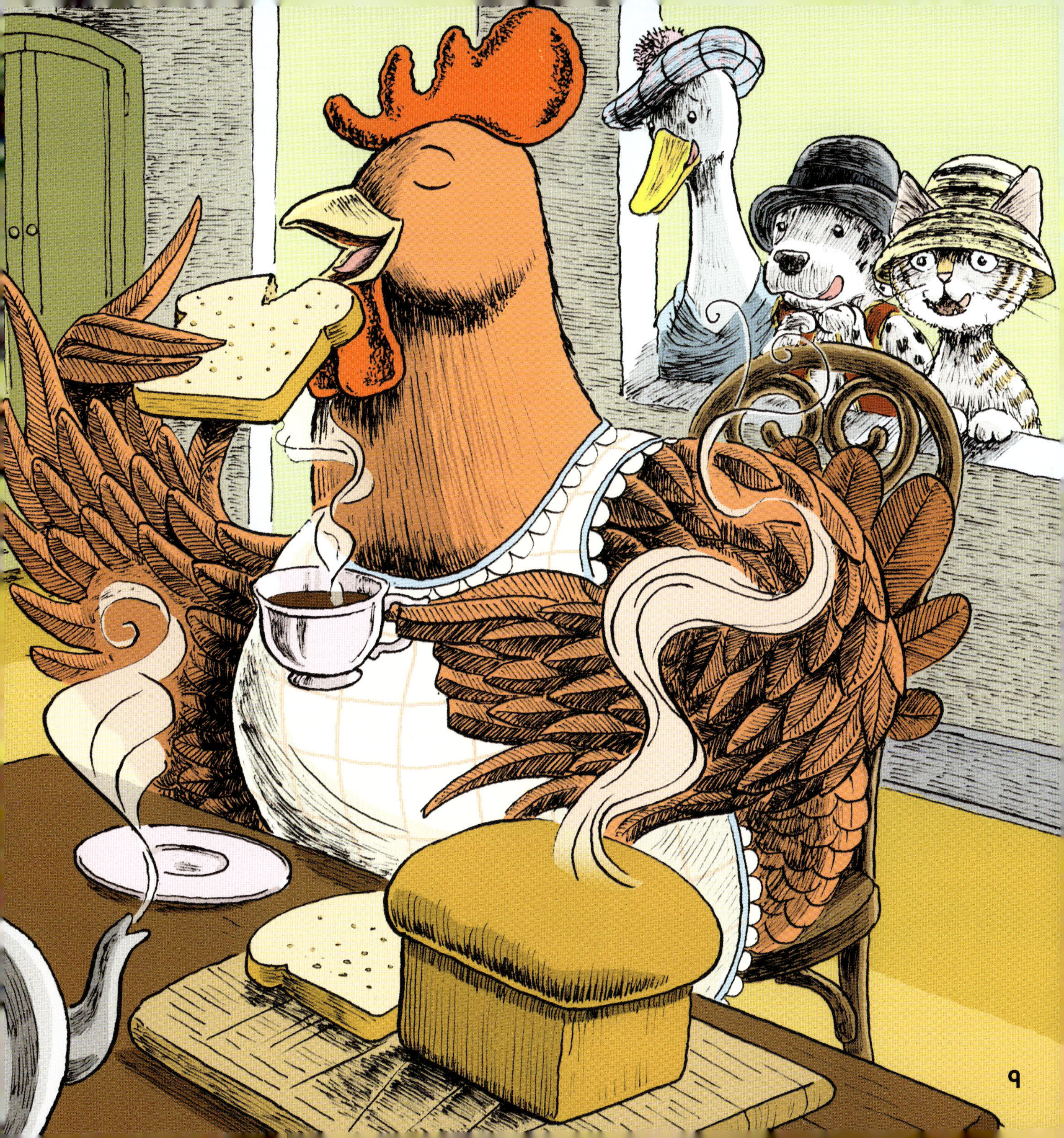

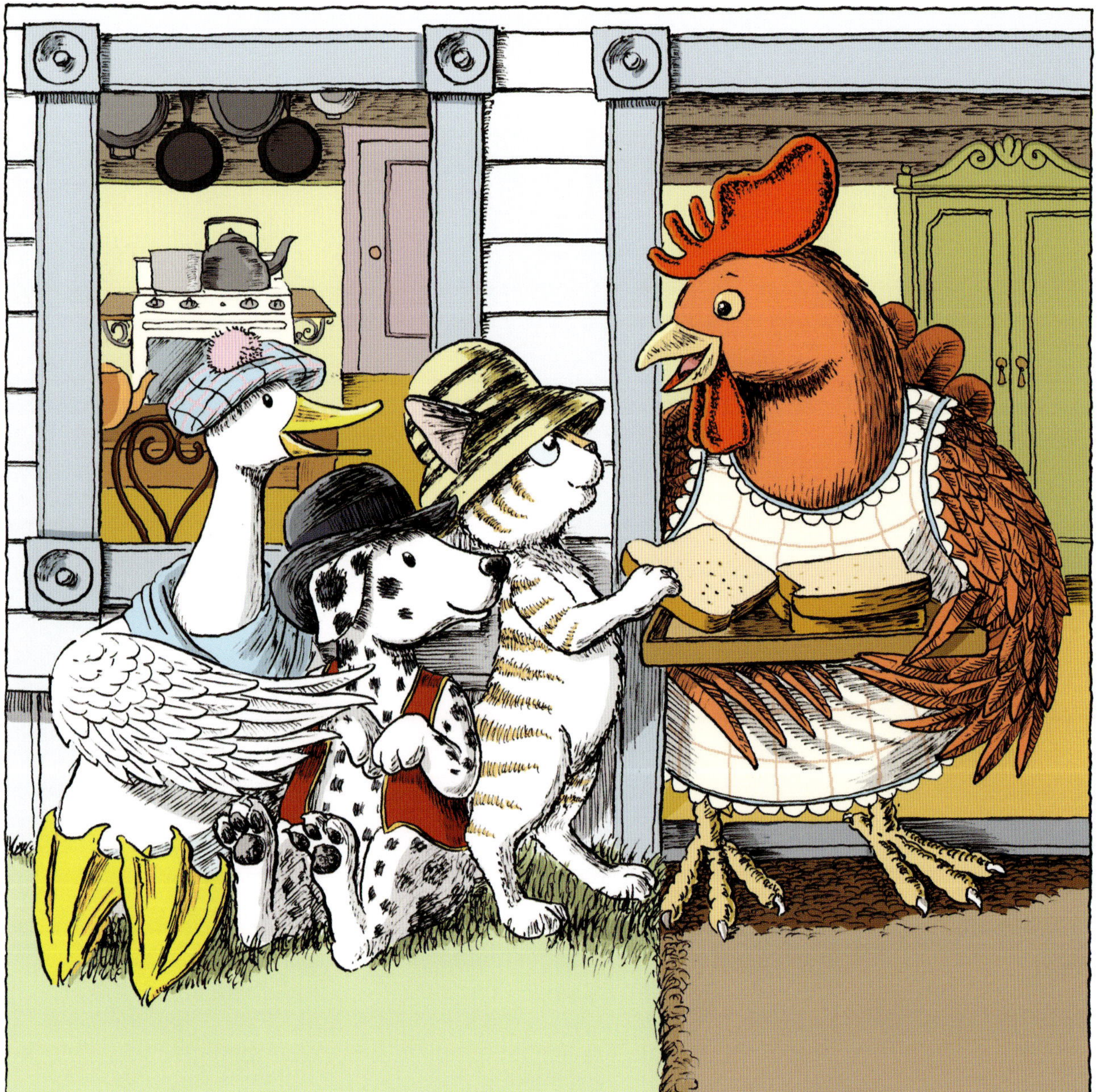

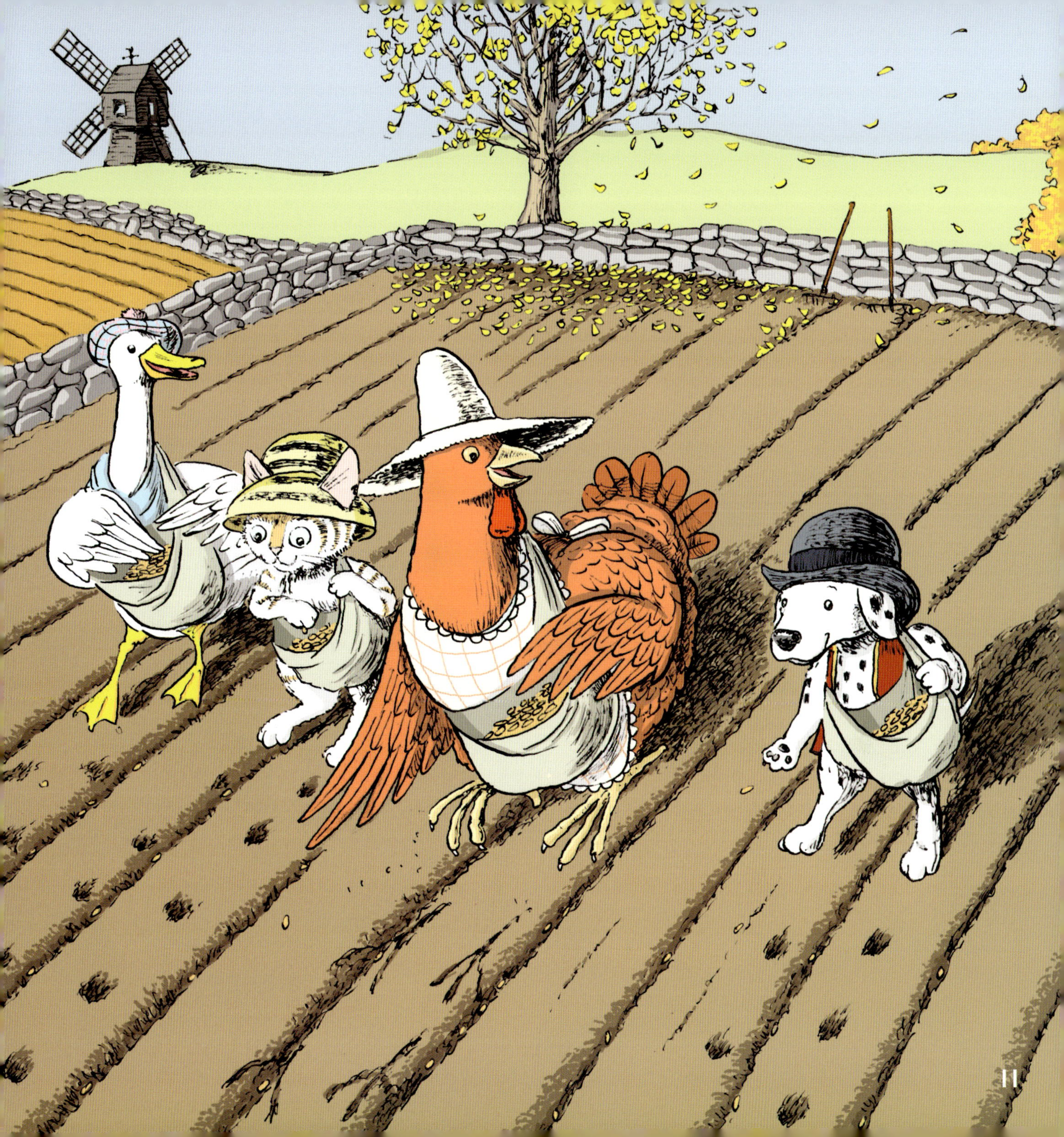

Retell the story

Once upon a time...

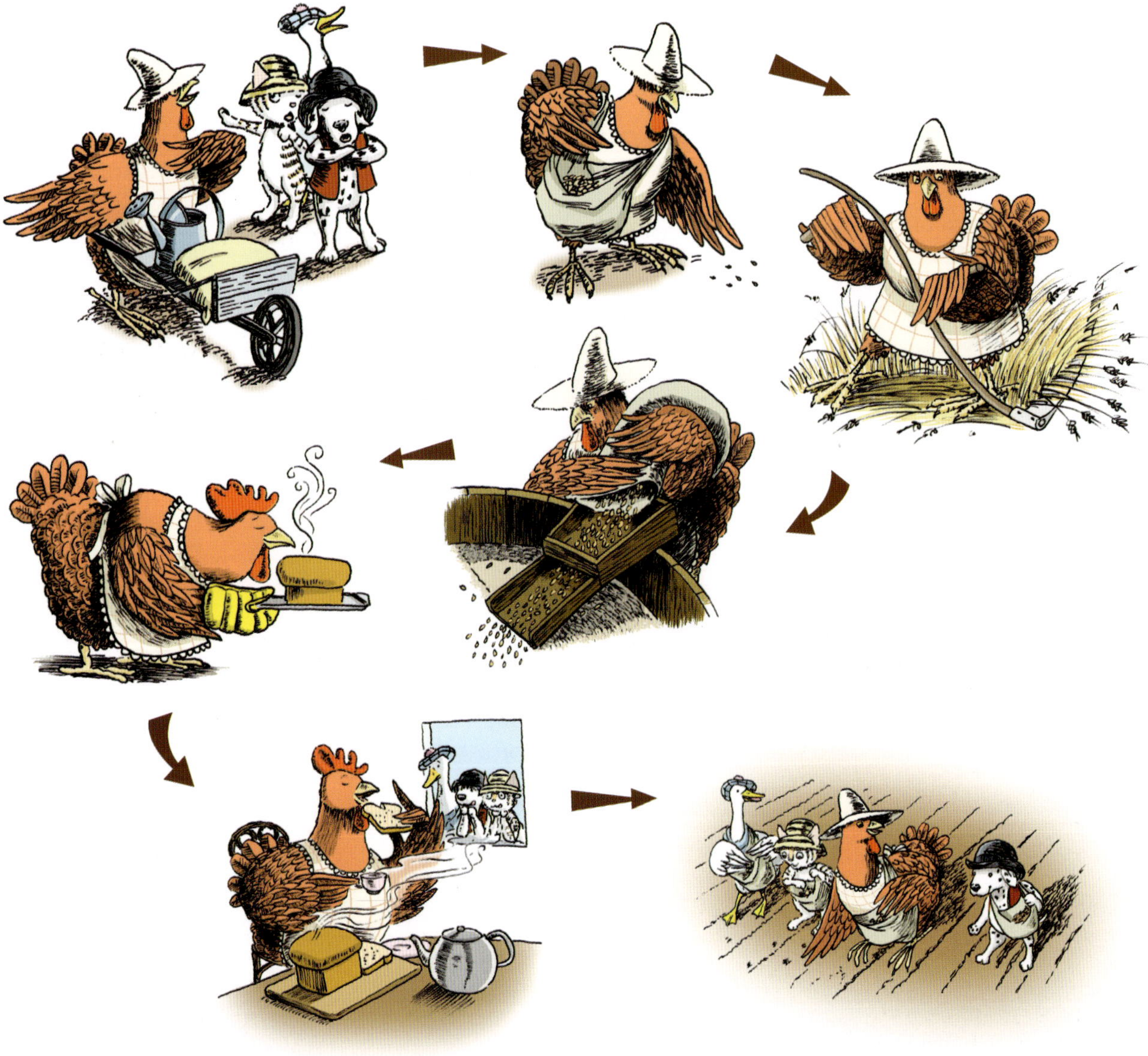

The end.